This book is dedicated to all six of my wonderful children ...
"a shout of joy comes in the morning."

—CA

To John for all of the encouragement ... Thanks Barney!

—RC

ZONDERKIDZ

The Legend of the Sand Dollar

Requests for information should be addressed to:

Zonderkidz, *3900 Sparks Drive SE, Grand Rapids, Michigan 49546*

ISBN 978-0-310-74980-6

Art direction and design: Kris Nelson

Printed in China

17 18 19 20 21 /DHC/ 21 20 19 18 17 16 15 14 13 12 11 10 9 8 7 6 5 4 3 2 1

The Legend of the Sand Dollar

An Inspirational Story of Hope for Easter

WRITTEN BY Chris Auer

ILLUSTRATED BY Richard Cowdrey

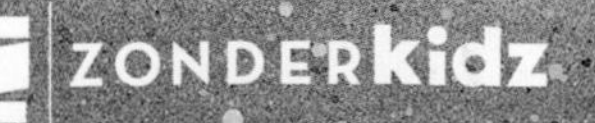

"Why can't Mom and Dad take us to the beach?" Kerry sniffled.

"It's only two days," whispered Margaret, "and they'll come get us on Easter morning."

Kerry tried not to cry. Every few years her family went to Aunt Jane's house near the beach. *I'll just think about playing with Cousin Jack,* she told herself. *I'll just think about the ocean.*

But her tears still fell as the bus took her farther and farther away from her mom and dad.

Early the next morning at Aunt Jane's, Kerry went out to look at the boats on the river.

Kerry still missed her parents, but soon she heard the *putt-putt-putt* of an engine coming toward her from upstream. Cousin Jack!

"Kerry!" Jack hollered.

“What do you think about my new boat?”

“It’s not very big,” she called back.

“Then it’s perfect for you!” He took her hand as she climbed on board.

The river opened to the wide bay.

"Hang on!" Jack yelled. Suddenly, the ocean lay before them, as broad as the sky. A small island appeared in the distance.

Waves lapped against the shore as Jack beached the boat.

"What's this?" Kerry called, holding up a round object.

"That's a sand dollar," Jack answered.

"A sand dollar?" Kerry cried. "This isn't money!"

"Right," said Jack. "It's a starfish that used to live in the ocean."

"How do they get here?" Kerry asked.

"When the tide goes out, it leaves sand dollars behind," Jack said.

"Why are they called dollars?" she asked.

"Real dollars used to be round," said Jack, "and they were made of silver. But sand dollars have value too."

"Then I guess we're rich," Kerry teased.

"In a way," he answered. "The sand dollar tells a story—the greatest story of all."

“Can you see the Easter lily on that side?
It’s like a trumpet saying, ‘Jesus is alive!’”

"Now look in the middle of the lily. There's the star from the East that led wise men to Christ. We remember Jesus' birth on this side too. See the Christmas flower?"

"Both sides of the sand dollar tell the Easter story. See the four nail holes—and a fifth hole made by a spear? These remind us that Jesus died for us."

"Now hold out your hand," said Jack, "and watch very carefully." He broke open one of the sand dollars, and five white shapes fluttered down.

"See the doves? This is the new life—the promise of Easter. As Jesus lives again, so can we. And these doves remind us to spread his promise and this hope to all people."

That night, the moon rose full across the water.

"You know what?" asked Jack. "Your parents aren't that far away—like the moon and the tide."

"But the moon is far away from the ocean," said Kerry.

"They're still connected," Jack explained. "The moon's gravity is what pulls the tide high."

"From that far away?"

"That's how the tide works."

"Like how God can remind us that he is close too," whispered Kerry, thinking of the sand dollar.

The next morning, Kerry put a sand dollar into her sister's hands.

"Happy Easter, Margaret," she said.

"Thanks, Kerry!"

Kerry smiled and asked, "Do you see the Easter lily?"

"An Easter lily?"

"Yeah, and inside there are little doves. I'll tell you the whole story."

As they waited for their parents, Kerry shared the good news with her sister.

Soon Margaret smiled too.

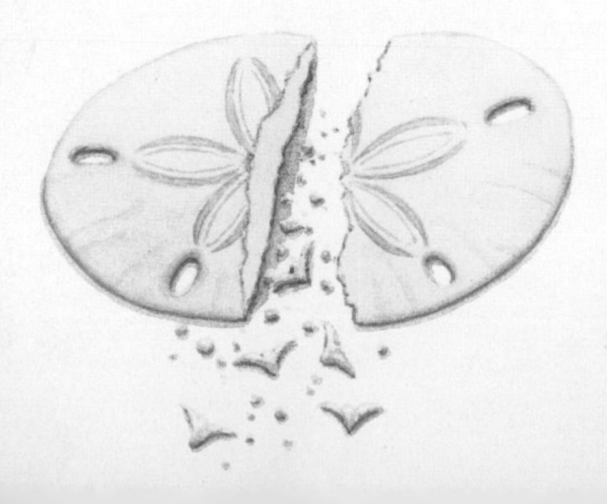

All about Sand Dollars

Sand dollar is the name for a marine animal that is related to the starfish. Sand dollars have flat, rigid, disk-shaped shells made of interlocked plates just beneath their skin.

Living sand dollars are fuzzy and brown or pinkish. They burrow in sand, feeding on small organic particles. Just their skeletons—or shells—wash onto beaches.

Only collect sand dollars that are no longer alive. They look like white coins and are about 1–4 inches (approx. 2.5–10 cm) in diameter. Sand dollars are easiest to find at low tide, along the edge of the receding water. The sand washes away from the buried shells as a wave goes out, and the next wave covers them with sand again.

In North America, people who live along the coastline often recite this popular poem about sand dollars:

There's a pretty little legend
That I would like to tell
Of the birth and death of Jesus
Found in this lowly shell.

If you examine closely,
You'll see that you find here
Four nail holes and a fifth one
Made by a Roman's spear.

On one side; the Easter lily.
It's center is the star
That appeared unto the shepherds
And led them from afar.

The Christmas poinsettia
Etched on the other side
Reminds us of his birthday,
Our happy Christmastide.

Now break the center open,
And here you will release
The five doves awaiting
To spread good will and peace.

This simple little symbol
Christ left for you and me
To help us spread his gospel
Through all eternity.

–Author Unknown